This book belongs to:

Disney PRINCESS

Beauty AND THE Beast

The Story of Belle

Disney PRINCESS

Beauty AND THE Beast

The Story of Belle

Disney PRESS

Los Angeles • New York

Published by Disney Press, an imprint of Disney Book Group. No part of this book may
be reproduced or transmitted in any form or by any means, electronic or mechanical,
including photocopying, recording, or by any information storage and retrieval system,
without written permission from the publisher. For information address Disney Press,
1101 Flower Street, Glendale, California 91201.

Printed in the United States of America
First Hardcover Edition, January 2016
3 5 7 9 10 8 6 4 2

Library of Congress Control Number: 2015947451
FAC-038091-15352
ISBN 978-1-4847-6720-7

disneybooks.com

*It's what's inside
that counts . . .*

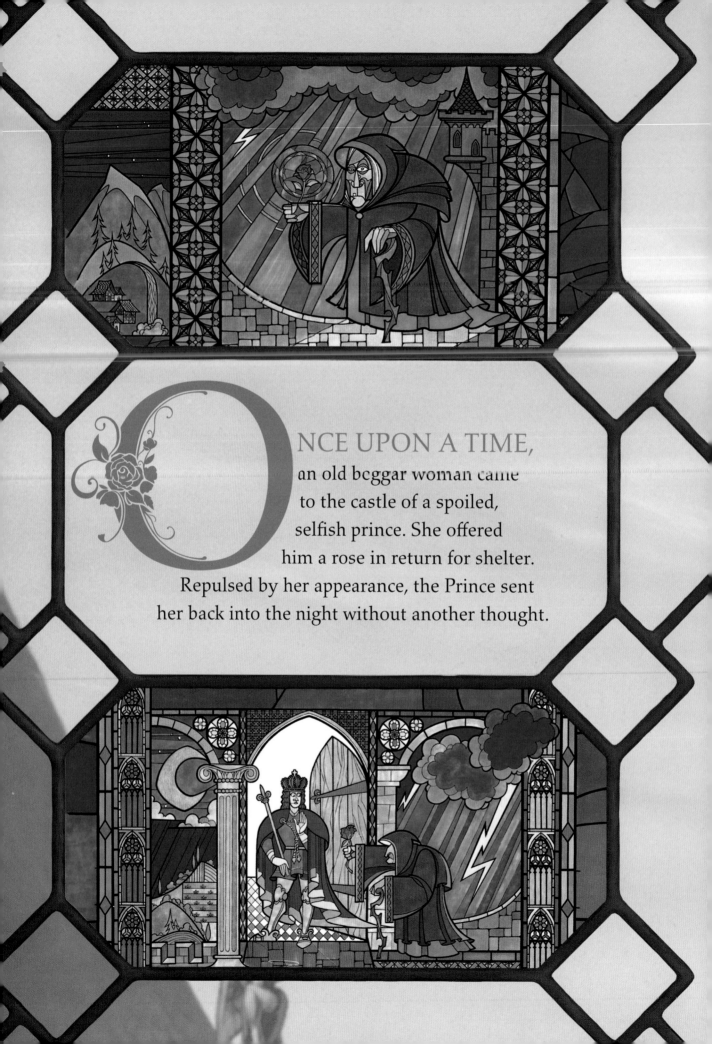

ONCE UPON A TIME, an old beggar woman came to the castle of a spoiled, selfish prince. She offered him a rose in return for shelter. Repulsed by her appearance, the Prince sent her back into the night without another thought.

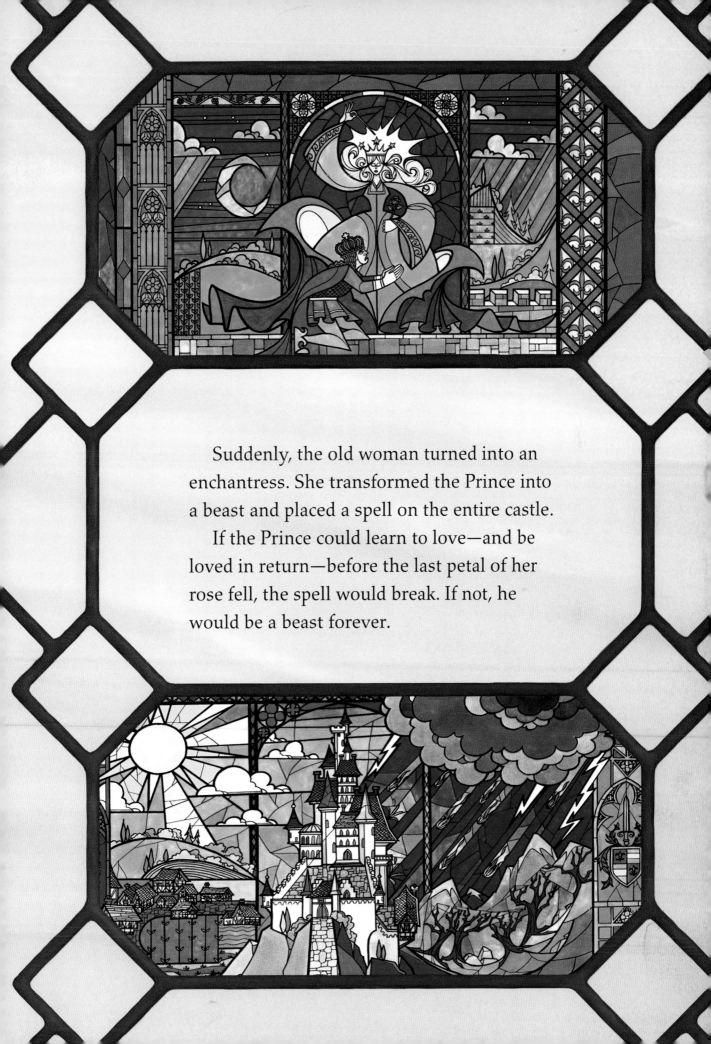

Suddenly, the old woman turned into an enchantress. She transformed the Prince into a beast and placed a spell on the entire castle.

If the Prince could learn to love—and be loved in return—before the last petal of her rose fell, the spell would break. If not, he would be a beast forever.

Not far away, a young woman named Belle dreamed about a more exciting life than what she found in her small village. She wanted adventures like those she read about in her beloved books.

Belle always had her nose in a book, so the villagers thought she was strange. But she was also very beautiful. That's why Gaston, the most handsome and conceited man in the village, wanted to marry her.

Gaston was certain that Belle would feel lucky to marry him. But Belle didn't want to marry such a boorish fellow—especially one who didn't appreciate her love of books.

"It's not right for a woman to read," said Gaston. "Soon she starts getting ideas, and thinking."

As Belle headed home, Gaston's sidekick, LeFou, laughed and called her father, Maurice, a crazy old loon. "My father's not crazy. He's a genius!" replied Belle. Then a loud *BANG!* came from her cottage, where Maurice was working on a new invention.

"I'll never get this boneheaded contraption to work!" Maurice said, kicking a piece of his new invention, an automatic wood chopper.

"Yes, you will," Belle said. "And you'll win first prize at the fair tomorrow."

With her encouragement, Maurice fixed his invention.

On his way to the fair, Maurice got lost, and his
horse, Phillipe, bolted in fear. All alone, Maurice was
surrounded by snarling wolves. To escape, he stumbled
through a huge gate.

Inside the gate was an enormous castle. Its shadowy
hall seemed empty, but Maurice heard whispering.
"Is someone there?" Maurice called. He picked up a
candelabrum to light his way.
"Hello!" the candelabrum answered.

Maurice couldn't believe his eyes! The castle was full of enchanted objects that could move and talk. They appeared to be servants in the house. The candelabrum, Lumiere, and the clock, Cogsworth, led Maurice to a comfortable chair, where he sat until . . .

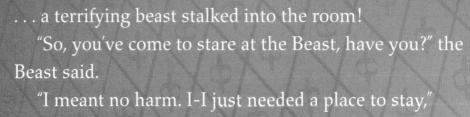

. . . a terrifying beast stalked into the room!

"So, you've come to stare at the Beast, have you?" the
Beast said.

"I meant no harm. I-I just needed a place to stay,"
Maurice stammered.

"I'll give you a place to stay," the Beast snapped. Then
he locked Maurice in the dungeon.

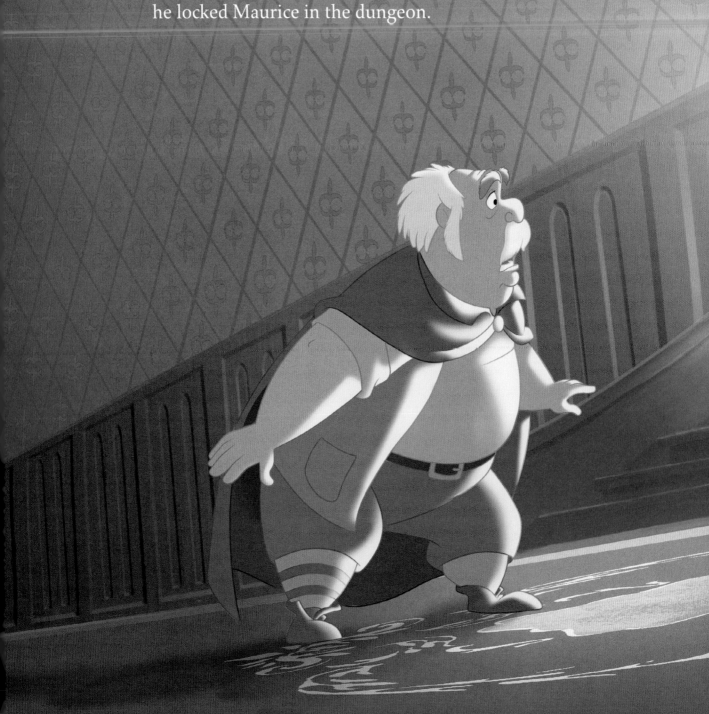

Meanwhile, Gaston had decided that the day of his wedding had arrived. He was sure Belle would marry him, so he had made all the preparations—except one. He hadn't bothered to propose yet.

Belle was surprised to see Gaston, but she was even more surprised when he announced that it was the day her dreams would come true: the day she would marry him!

"I'm very sorry, Gaston, but I just don't deserve you," Belle replied. Gaston leaned against the door just as she opened it.

SPLAT! Gaston tumbled out the door and into a mud puddle.

LeFou stopped conducting the wedding band to check on Gaston. Furious, Gaston shouted, "I'll have Belle for my wife. Make no mistake about that!"

Belle ran to a nearby field to clear her head, and soon
Phillipe galloped to join her. She was alarmed to see
him alone.

"Where's Papa? What happened?" Belle asked the
horse. "You have to take me to him!"

It was growing dark by the time Belle and Phillipe arrived at the castle gate. Belle peered inside and saw Maurice's hat lying on the path. Determined to find her father, she entered the dark castle.

But when Belle discovered Maurice in the dungeon, the Beast lunged from the shadows.

"What are you doing here?" he roared.

Belle pleaded for the Beast to take her instead of Maurice.

The Beast accepted, with one condition. "You must promise to stay here forever," he said.

Now free, Maurice raced back to town, shouting for
help to rescue Belle from a horrible beast.
    But everyone laughed at "crazy old Maurice."
Everyone except Gaston. He had just thought of a way
to use Maurice to force Belle into marriage.

Back at the castle, Belle met some of the enchanted servants, including Mrs. Potts, a kind teapot, and her son, a cute teacup named Chip.

"That was a very brave thing you did, my dear," said Mrs. Potts. She knew that Belle had chosen to stay in the castle to save Maurice.

Belle shook her head. "But I've lost my father, my dreams, everything."

Downstairs, the Beast was furious because Belle had refused to join him for dinner. "If she doesn't eat with me, then she doesn't eat at all!" he roared at the servants.

"Try to act like a gentleman," Mrs. Potts advised him.

Later that night, when Belle grew hungry, she crept
down to the kitchen for a bite to eat.

To her delight, the staff treated her to a feast with
singing and dancing! They were thrilled to finally have
a guest.

After dinner, Belle wanted to explore the castle. The
Beast had forbidden her to go into the West Wing,
which made her curious. Cogsworth and Lumiere tried
to discourage her, but Belle slipped away from them and
ventured up the stairs.

Belle entered a darkened room and gasped at the ripped curtains and broken furniture. Then she saw a rose glowing under a glass dome. Several petals had fallen. Entranced by its beauty, she reached out. But before she could touch it . . .

. . . the Beast burst into the room!

"I warned you never to come here!" he bellowed. "Do you realize what you could have done? Get out!"

Terrified, Belle ran from the castle. "Promise or no promise, I can't stay here another minute!" she cried. She found Phillipe outside, and the two raced into the forest. But soon ferocious wolves surrounded them!

Before the wolves could attack Belle and Phillipe, the Beast sprang from the shadows. Growling and snarling, he fought off the wolves' snapping jaws. At last, the pack fled, howling, into the woods.

But the Beast had been hurt. Belle tended to his wounds.

"If you hadn't run away, this wouldn't have happened," the Beast said.

"If you hadn't frightened me, I wouldn't have run away," Belle replied. Then she added, "Thank you for saving my life."

"You're welcome," said the Beast.

Meanwhile, Gaston, followed by LeFou, met Monsieur D'Arque from the Asylum de Loons and bribed him to declare Maurice insane. Belle's father would be locked up in the asylum—unless Belle agreed to marry Gaston!

As the days passed, Belle saw a gentle and kind
side of the Beast. The birds, too, noticed a difference,
and they perched fearlessly on his shoulders and ate
birdseed from his paws.

The staff watched the couple hopefully. Even Chip knew something
special was happening.

It seemed as if Belle and the Beast were beginning to care for each
other. Perhaps—just perhaps—the spell would finally be broken and
everyone would become human again.

One evening, the Beast arranged an elegant dinner and asked Belle to join him. That time she accepted. The Beast tried very hard to act like a gentleman, and Belle was impressed.

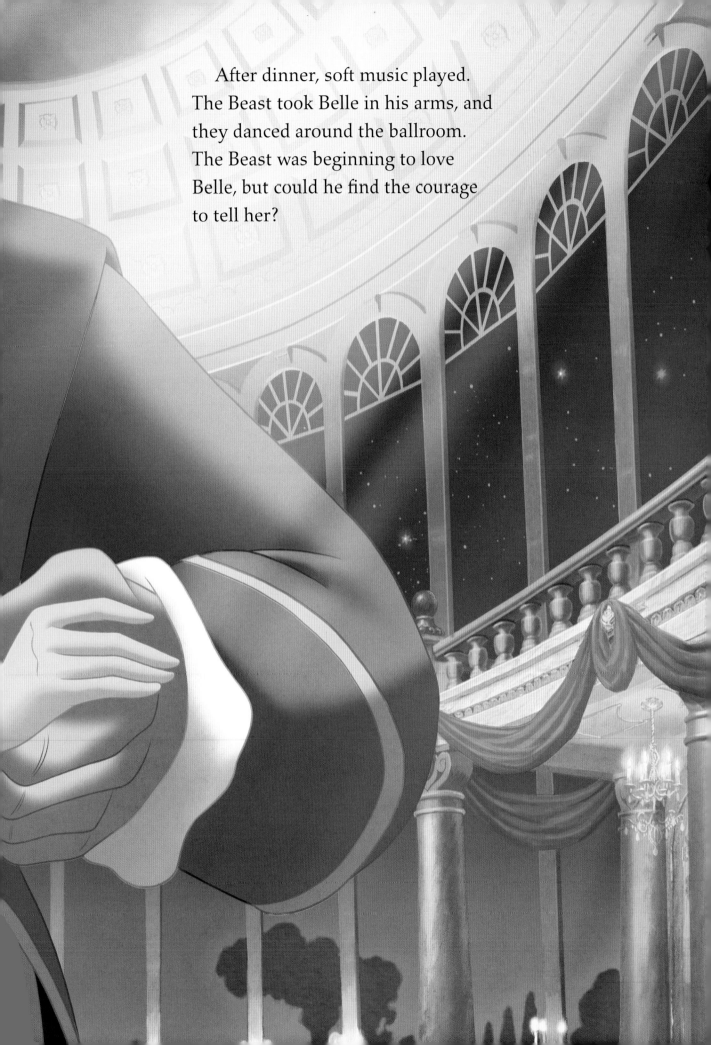

After dinner, soft music played. The Beast took Belle in his arms, and they danced around the ballroom. The Beast was beginning to love Belle, but could he find the courage to tell her?

The Beast asked Belle if she was happy. She replied that she was but she missed her father. So the Beast showed her a magic mirror that revealed an image of Maurice. He was in trouble.

Although there was little time left to break the curse, the Beast released Belle from her promise, letting her go find her father.

The Beast gave Belle the mirror so she would
remember him. But as he watched her ride away, he
howled in pain. He loved her and would miss her, and
worse still, it seemed that any hope of breaking the
spell was gone forever.

Belle rushed Maurice home after finding him. To their surprise, Chip had snuck into her bag and come along, too.

"How did you escape that horrible beast?" asked Maurice.

"He's different now, Papa," Belle said. But before she could explain, there was a knock at the door.

Monsieur D'Arque had arrived to take Maurice away!
As the guards dragged Maurice to the asylum wagon,
Gaston cornered Belle. "I might be able to clear up this
little misunderstanding," he said, "*if* you marry me."
"Never!" Belle exclaimed.

To prove that her father wasn't crazy, Belle showed the villagers the Beast's image in the enchanted mirror. "He's really kind and gentle. He's my friend," she told them.

Jealous and enraged, Gaston seized the mirror. "Kill the Beast!" he shouted. Then Gaston locked Belle and Maurice in their cottage and led the townspeople, with torches blazing, to the castle.

As the mob approached, Mrs. Potts ran to the Beast, alarmed.

"What shall we do, master?" she asked.

But with Belle gone, the Beast no longer cared about anything. "Just let them come," he said.

The servants were left to think of a plan on their own.

With a crash, the castle doors flew open, and the townspeople stormed inside. But the servants were ready!

The hat rack punched, the wardrobe slammed her doors, and the chairs kicked. At last, the servants chased the townspeople away.

Only Gaston remained. Finding the Beast alone, he raised his bow.

The Beast did not fight back. When Gaston's arrow hit him, he staggered, then crashed through the window and tumbled onto the castle roof.

Gaston followed the Beast. "Get up!" he shouted. "What's the matter? Too kind and gentle to fight back?"

Gaston raised a club, but before he could strike, Belle screamed from below, "No!" She and Maurice had escaped from the cottage and raced to the castle.

At the sound of Belle's voice, hope filled the Beast's heart and gave him the will to defend himself. He lunged at Gaston and held him near the roof's edge.

"Let me go! Please, don't hurt me," begged the bully.

The Beast had changed. He no
longer wanted to hurt anyone—not
even Gaston. He released Gaston
and climbed to a terrace, where Belle
had run to meet him.

But Gaston surprised them and
stabbed the Beast.

The Beast roared with pain and whipped around, startling Gaston, who slipped and fell. With a cry, Gaston plunged through the darkness toward the rocks below.

Belle pulled the Beast to safety and knelt beside him.

"You came back," he whispered. "At least I got to see you one last time."

"Please don't leave me," Belle sobbed. "I love you."

As she spoke, the last rose petal
fell. Then, suddenly, magical sparkles
began to swirl around the Beast. He
rose into the air, turning slowly in
a shower of light. Belle watched in
disbelief as the Beast transformed.

He became a handsome prince!
"Belle!" he cried. "It's me!"
Belle gazed into the Prince's eyes.
"It *is* you!" she said.

Magic swirled above the castle. Happy cries rang out as the servants transformed back into their human selves. The spell was broken!

"It is a miracle!" Lumiere shouted.

But no one was more joyful than Belle and her prince. The servants watched them waltz across the ballroom.

"Are they gonna live happily ever after, Mama?" Chip asked.

"Of course, my dear," Mrs. Potts replied.

And they did.

To be continued . . .